AF559682

Birbal & the Cannibals

Books by Delshad Karanjia

Teaching a Horse to Sing: Tales of Uncommon Sense from India and Elsewhere
Akbar and Birbal: The Finest Stories of the Emperor and His Wise Minister

{450}

Birbal & the Cannibals

FOUR TALES OF AKBAR AND BIRBAL

DELSHAD KARANJIA

Illustrations by Mohit Suneja

ALEPH

ALEPH BOOK COMPANY
An independent publishing firm
promoted by ***Rupa Publications India***

First published in India in 2025
by Aleph Book Company
7/16 Ansari Road, Daryaganj
New Delhi 110 002

This is a work of fiction. Names, characters, places, and incidents are either the product of the author's imagination or are used fictitiously and any resemblance to any actual persons, living or dead, events, or locales is entirely coincidental.

ISBN: 978-93-6523-360-5

1 3 5 7 9 10 8 6 4 2

Printed in India

For the Best

While hunting deer in a dense forest several miles away from Fatehpur Sikri, Akbar and Birbal somehow became separated from the rest of the hunting party. After riding for several hours, calling for help in the vain hope that the royal entourage was within earshot, the emperor and his trusted adviser had to accept that they were hopelessly lost.

Tired and thirsty, their mashq empty, the duo decided to give their horses a rest in a shady spot under a canopy of trees. Akbar was incensed that his attendants had failed to keep up with him. 'This is the height of incompetence,' he fumed. 'How on earth did my courtiers manage to lose sight of me?'

'Everything happens for the best, huzoor,' said Birbal calmly. 'Don't you recall that about twenty years ago you were in a similar predicament in a forest near Agra where we met for the first time? There are always hidden forces at work that steer us on the right path. Let us ride on further until we reach a river or lake.'

'What is the use of ruling an empire that boasts a hundred rivers if I cannot get a drink of water when I need it?' Akbar muttered as they rode on.

'Be patient, My Lord, it will be for the best,' Birbal repeated.

Irritated by Birbal's optimism, the emperor rode on in stony silence, his wazir by his side, until they suddenly spotted a small well a short distance away. Reining in their horses, Akbar ordered Birbal to get him a drink of water from the well.

'Your wish is my command,' Birbal said, dismounting and heading for the well with his mashq. Behind him, Akbar dismounted from his steed and started to follow Birbal, but tripped on a small rock and fell headlong, managing to break his fall with both hands. Hearing the emperor calling out in pain, Birbal rushed to his assistance. Akbar's palms were badly grazed and bleeding, and the only thing Birbal could do to help was pour water from his mashq to clean and soothe the emperor's injuries.

'What a calamitous day this is turning out to be,' Akbar grumbled, dabbing at his bleeding palms with the edge of his silk turban, which had come undone when he fell.

'Everything happens for the best. I'm certain some good will come out of these mishaps,' Birbal said.

'Birbal, that is a ridiculous and insensitive thing to say when you can see that I am hurt and in pain. This is neither the time nor the place for your platitudes. Take your horse and get out of my sight,' Akbar said angrily. Thinking it best not to argue, Birbal took his horse by the reins and walked off into the dense forest ahead of them.

As Akbar raised the mashq to his lips to take a sip of water, he heard a rustling sound behind him and realized that he was not alone. Veering around, he saw four fierce-looking tribesmen with white streaks painted on their faces and across their bare chests, pointing their sharp spears at him.

The leader of the tribesmen approached Akbar slowly and said: 'I am Zofar, chief of the cannibals. You have trespassed into our land. Now we must sacrifice you to our god and then feast on you.'

Holding up his hands with palms facing outwards, to keep the cannibals at bay, Akbar said: 'I am Emperor Akbar of Hindustan. All this land belongs to me, so it is you who are trespassing. I can order my soldiers to execute each one of you.'

The painted tribesmen did not pay much heed to the emperor's threats but were staring at his bleeding hands. Zofar took a step back and said: 'It would be an affront to our god to offer you as a sacrifice. It is forbidden to sacrifice injured persons or animals to the gods. Your bleeding hands have saved your life. We'll have to find something else for our dinner.' All four men turned around and vanished into the thick forest.

Relieved at his narrow escape, Akbar waited until the tribesmen had moved out of earshot, and began calling out to Birbal, who had hidden behind a tree and witnessed the emperor's encounter with the tribesmen. Apologizing profusely for banishing him, Akbar added: 'Birbal, as always, you were right. At least in my case, everything did happen for the best.'

Birbal replied: 'Hidden forces were

at work for me too, Jahanpanah. Your injured palms saved your life, and being banished into the woods saved mine. If I had been here with you, I would have ended up being the cannibals' dinner.'

Akbar looked shocked at the thought of Birbal ending up in a cauldron, and started to feel a little better about evicting him. 'Ultimately,' concluded Birbal, 'it is fate that determines whether one man's good fortune should mean misfortune for another.'

Breaking a Friendship

Akbar's son Prince Salim's childhood had been very different from that of his father's, who had spent his early years living in exile and in the care of aunts and other relatives. Salim, on the other hand, had been brought up in the lap of luxury, his every whim indulged by his parents and everyone around him.

At seventeen, the age at which his

father had already been emperor for three years, Prince Salim shouldered no responsibilities but preferred whiling away his time with his best friend, Harivansh, the son of a wealthy merchant. Both teenagers spent hours in each other's company, ignoring their tutors and duties, playing cards or chess instead.

One day, Harivansh's father approached Birbal for help. 'Huzoor,' the merchant said, 'my only son and Prince Salim are very close friends. I am not opposed to their friendship but feel that it should not be my son's main focus. The prince will one day become the ruler of Hindustan whether he has learned anything or not. But my son will

have to work for his living, and he will not succeed if he doesn't learn how to manage the business. My wealth won't last forever, and I'm worried about my son's future if he doesn't master my trade.'

'Don't worry,' Birbal reassured the merchant, 'I'll sort things out.'

When Birbal mentioned the merchant's concerns to the emperor, Akbar said: 'The queen and I too are worried about their friendship. The queen thinks Harivansh is a bad influence on Salim and should be banished from the kingdom. She wants to send Salim to live with her parents for a few months, but I don't think that will help. Salim needs to stay here and learn the art of statecraft. Harivansh is only required to manage his small business, which anyone can do. But Salim will have to govern an entire kingdom and must do so wisely and well.'

'Huzoor, what is your hukum? Do you want me to try and end their friendship?'

'I know it is never a good thing to break up a friendship, but I think in this case it will be the best thing for them both,' Akbar said, rubbing his chin.

That evening, Birbal dropped in to Prince Salim's quarters, and found the two friends lounging on a divan playing cards. Birbal made small talk with Salim for a few minutes and then turning to Harivansh, he said: 'Come here,

Harivansh. I need to talk to you about something highly confidential.' Birbal put an arm around Harivansh's shoulder, led him to a distant corner of the room and whispered something in the boy's ear. Harivansh looked puzzled but before he could speak, Birbal walked out of the room, saying: 'Please don't tell anyone what I told you.'

Salim was overcome with curiosity. 'What did he say? Tell me what he said,' he urged his friend.

'I couldn't make any sense of what he said,' Harivansh replied.

'How dare you lie to me! With my own two ears I heard Birbal say that he was telling you something in confidence.

I'm supposed to be your best friend, and this is how you treat me?' Salim said indignantly.

'You are my dearest friend, Salim, but please believe me—I couldn't make any sense of what Birbal mumbled in my ear. I think he said something like "even the smallest river flows into the mighty ocean". It made no sense at all.'

'Liar! You are making this up and hiding the truth from me,' Salim yelled angrily. 'Why would Birbal tell you something so idiotic and ask you not to tell anyone? If you cannot confide in me, it means that I cannot trust you and we cannot be friends.'

'You're an arrogant fool,' Harivansh

shouted back, 'because you don't believe the truth. I cannot be friends with someone who doesn't trust me.'

Prince Salim and Harivansh never spoke to each other again, and while the merchant's son went on to master his father's trade, the prince eventually ascended the throne as Emperor Jahangir, but was unable to attain his father's glorious heights.

Birbal Proves His Worth

His courtiers' jealousy of Birbal had become so routine that Akbar invariably chose to ignore their grumbling and complaints.

One day, when word reached him about a smarmy courtier's attempt to make a joke of the emperor's confidence in a country bumpkin who lived by his wits and was not half as clever as he made himself out to be, Akbar decided to put an end to the protests and backbiting once and for all.

'Since you are all against Birbal, I will leave it to you to sort out the next challenge that presents itself in my court,' the emperor told his courtiers. 'Birbal will stay out of it.'

The opportunity arose a few days later, when a stranger presented himself at Akbar's court one morning and introduced himself as a polyglot fluent in more than fifteen languages. 'Jahanpanah, I can speak many languages including Hindi, Urdu, Persian, Telugu, Tamil, Kannada, Marathi, Malayalam, Gujarati, Bengali, Odia, Punjabi, and others, each

one as fluently as if it were my native tongue. I have travelled for many days to reach your durbar, and I'd like to put the wise men of your court to the test to see if they can identify where I am from, and which of the languages is my mother tongue.'

Impressed by the scholar's confidence, Akbar readily accepted the challenge. His courtiers hailed from all over Hindustan and its neighbouring countries, and one or other of them would definitely be able to figure out where the multilingual scholar was from. Birbal was to play no part in unravelling the mystery. For the entire day, one by one, each courtier spoke in his mother tongue with the stranger, who responded with the fluency of a native speaker. The scholar was so well acquainted with the poetry and prose of every one of the languages, that each of the courtiers was convinced that he hailed from his part of the country. They couldn't all be right, and not wanting to be proved wrong, the courtiers eventually admitted that they were unable to pinpoint the scholar's origins.

Akbar was about to give his courtiers a tongue-lashing, when Birbal came to their rescue. 'Jahanpanah,' he said, 'this has been a time-consuming exercise for the courtiers, and it is quite late. Let's offer our visitor hospitality for the night and resume the challenge tomorrow.' The stranger was taken to the royal guest house, where he enjoyed a lavish meal before going to bed.

In a deep sleep after his tiring day, the scholar woke with a start when he heard loud banging sounds behind his bed. In the pitch dark, in an unfamiliar room, unable to make out what was causing the noise, the bewildered scholar jumped out of bed and ran out of the room calling for help. Finding Birbal standing in the corridor, the stranger explained what had happened. Birbal calmed him down: 'There's nothing to worry about. Your window was left unlatched, and is banging against the frame because of the wind. You can safely go back to bed but make sure you latch the window first.'

The next morning, the scholar returned to court to thank the emperor

for his hospitality before continuing on his journey. Before he could speak, Birbal stepped forward and declared: 'Your Majesty, we are honoured to have in our midst a man of great learning and

erudition. It is not often that one comes across a person who can speak so many languages so fluently. I am certain that he comes from Gujarat and his native language is Gujarati.'

Birbal's announcement took everyone by surprise, not least the courtiers and especially the scholar. With folded hands, the scholar bowed to Akbar and then to Birbal. 'I am indeed a Gujarati,' he said. 'For the past thirty years I have travelled across the length and breadth of Hindustan and no one has been able to identify my mother tongue. Your educated and well-spoken courtiers tested me for the entire day yesterday but could not do so either. I'm amazed that Huzoor

Birbal guessed correctly.'

'Tell us how you figured it out, Birbal,' Akbar commanded.

'I gave the matter some thought and came to the conclusion that when multilingual people feel fearful or panicky, they would instinctively speak in their first language...their mother tongue. Last night, when our guest was sleeping soundly, I repeatedly banged the window of his room rather loudly. Our guest woke up frightened and confused and rushed out of the room shouting in Gujarati, "What's going on? What's happening? God, please help me." And that's how I identified his native tongue.'

Akbar turned to face his courtiers. 'The

charge of favouritism towards Birbal that you levy against me is blatantly false. I think you have seen for yourselves why I value Birbal so highly. He managed to figure out where our visitor was from without even conversing with him. He manages to solve mysteries that perplex all of you, even though he occasionally resorts to unconventional methods to do so. An adviser such as Birbal is worth his weight in gold to a king.'

Meanwhile, the scholar, adequately compensated for the inconvenience that had been imposed on him the night before, continued his travels around the country, singing the praises of the emperor and his wazir in a multiplicity of languages.

The Art Competition

Renowned for being a patron of the arts, Akbar's court was an open house for writers, poets, musicians, dancers, sculptors, and artists. Now and again, the emperor would issue a challenge to each of these groups and present a lucrative reward to the winner.

To appease his brother-in-law, Raja Jaimal, who was still sulking for being deposed from his post as adviser, Akbar decided to hold an art competition, and appointed Raja Jaimal and Birbal to judge the works of art and select one entry each. Akbar would decide the winner and award a purse of gold coins to the artist who painted the best picture depicting peace.

Artists from the emperor's courts in Delhi, Agra, and Fatehpur Sikri submitted an extraordinary array of paintings—blissful portraits of mothers and children, sleeping babies, priests at prayer, people meditating, doves flying, swans gliding in lotus ponds, flowers blooming, idyllic landscapes, and so on.

Jaimal scrutinized the submissions

and finally picked his favourite. It was a serene depiction of a peaceful lake, whose crystal-clear waters perfectly mirrored the towering mountains surrounding it. Above the majestic forested peaks was a pale-blue sky dotted with fluffy white clouds. Everyone who saw it thought it was a perfect representation of peace. It appeared to be the top choice of the courtiers.

The painting selected by Birbal was also a landscape of mountains, but these were craggy and bare. Above them was a sky covered with dark clouds from which rain fell accompanied by bolts of lightning. In the forefront of the painting there was a cascading waterfall

that ended in swirls of foam. It wasn't exactly the kind of picture one would think of as depicting serenity. When the emperor and his courtiers looked at the painting more closely, they saw a tiny shrub growing out of a crevice in the rock beside the waterfall. A bird had built her nest in that bush, and within a few feet of the angry torrent of water pouring down beside her, the mother bird was sitting on her eggs in the nest in perfect peace.

Puzzled by Birbal's choice of painting, Akbar thought it best to give both judges a chance to explain their selections.

For once, Raja Jaimal was brief: 'I

chose this landscape because it is an embodiment of peace and tranquillity. One feels calmer merely by looking at it. Need I say more?'

Now it was Birbal's turn. 'Most Serene Majesty,' he began, 'I picked this painting because I have a different philosophy about peace. To my mind, peace does not imply a place where there is no noise, no danger, no discord. Real peace means being in the midst of all these things and still having the ability to be calm at heart. True peace comes from within us. That is the real meaning of peace. That tiny bird sitting serenely in her nest despite all the turmoil around her is a true embodiment of peace.'

Akbar awarded the prize money to Birbal's choice, and the fickle courtiers applauded. All except Raja Jaimal, who had got it wrong once again.